'Twas the Night Before THANKSGIVING

Story and Pictures by DAV PILKEY

SCHOLASTIC INC.

New York Toronto London Auckland Sydney
Mexico City New Delhi Hong Kong Buenos Aires

This book was originally published in hardcover by Orchard Books in 1990.

ISBN-13: 978-0-439-66937-5
ISBN-10: 0-439-66937-5

Published by Orchard Books, an imprint of Scholastic Inc. ORCHARD BOOKS and design are registered trademarks of Watts Publishing Group, Ltd., used under license. SCHOLASTIC and associated logos are trademarks and/or registered trademarks of Scholastic Inc.

12 11 10 9   8 9 10 11 12/0

Printed in the U.S.A.   40
First Bookshelf edition, October 2004
Book design by Mina Greenstein

For Cyndi and Nate

"...And what is done with love is well done."
—VINCENT VAN GOGH

'Twas the day before Thanksgiving
And all through the trees,
The fall leaves were spinning
Aloft in the breeze.

Eight children had boarded
Their school bus with grins
In hopes that a field trip
Soon would begin.

They sang as they rode
Through autumn terrains,
While visions of drumsticks
Danced in their brains.

O'er rivers, through woods,
With winding and weaves,
Their school bus sailed on
Through the new-fallen leaves.

When out on the road
There arose such a clatter,
They threw down their windows
To see what was the matter.

When what with their wondering eyes
Should they see,
But a miniature farm
And eight tiny turkey.

And a little old man
So lively and rugged,
They knew in a moment
It was Farmer Mack Nuggett.

He was dressed all in denim
From his head to his toe,
With a pinch of polyester
And a dash of Velcro.

And then in a twinkling
They heard in the straw
The prancing and pawing
Of each little claw.

More rapid than chickens
His cockerels they came.
He whistled and shouted
And called them by name:

"Now Ollie, now Stanley, now Larry and Moe,
On Wally, on Beaver, on Shemp and Groucho!"

The turkeys were chunky
With smiley, beaked faces,
And they greeted the children
With downy embraces.

So out through the barnyard
They ran and they flew,
And they gobbled and giggled
As friends sometimes do.

Then somebody spotted
An ax by the door,
And she asked Farmer Nuggett
What it was for.

With a blink of his eye
And a twist of his head,
The old farmer told
A grim tale of dread:

"Tonight," said Mack Nuggett,
"These feathery beasts
  Will be chopped up and roasted
  For Thanksgiving feasts."

The children stood still
As tears filled their eyes,
Then they clamored aloud
In a chorus of cries.

"Oh dear," cried Mack Nuggett,
"Now what shall I do?"
So he dashed to the well,
And the teacher went, too.

And they fetched some water
Fresh from the ground,
In hopes that a swig
Might calm everyone down.

And when they returned
To quiet the matter,
The children were calmer
(And mysteriously fatter!).

The boys and girls drank up
Their drinks in the hay,
Then thanked old Mack Nuggett
And waddled away.

They limped to the school bus
All huffing and puffing—
It's not easy to walk
With hot turkey stuffing.

And then, as the school bus drove off in the night,
Mack Nuggett looked 'round—not a turkey in sight!

'Twas the night before Thanksgiving,
And the stars up above
Shone down on a school bus
Abounding with love.

The very next evening,
Eight families were blessed
With eight fluffy
    Thanksgiving turkeys
As guests.

They feasted on veggies
With jelly and toast,
And everyone was thankful
(The turkeys were most!).

So each one gave thanks
For love and for living,
And they all had a wonderful
Happy Thanksgiving.